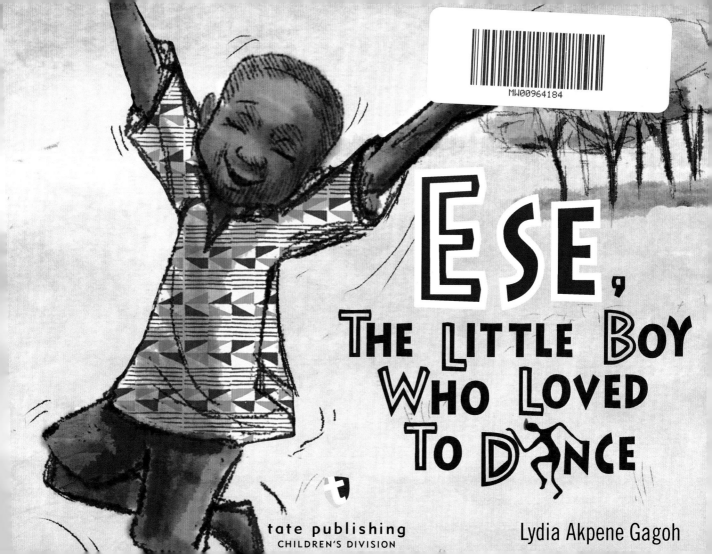

Ese,
THE LITTLE BOY WHO LOVED TO DANCE

tate publishing
CHILDREN'S DIVISION

Lydia Akpene Gagoh

Published by Tate Publishing & Enterprises, LLC
127 E. Trade Center Terrace | Mustang, Oklahoma 73064 USA
1.888.361.9473 | www.tatepublishing.com

Tate Publishing is committed to excellence in the publishing industry. The company reflects the philosophy established by the founders, based on Psalm 68:11,
"The Lord gave the word and great was the company of those who published it."

Book design copyright © 2012 by Tate Publishing, LLC. All rights reserved.
Cover and interior design by James Mensidor
Illustrations by Samantha Kickingbird

Published in the United States of America

ISBN: 978-1-62295-072-0
Juvenile Fiction / Performing Arts / Dance
13.03.05

Dedication

To my children Ese, Joshua, Precious, Olivia, and Hannah—you inspire me!
And to Dr. Kwame Osei Atuah—this is the first of many books.

Acknowledgments

Special thanks to my friends Lori, Linda, Meghan, Robin, Julia, and Kara.

Let everything that has breath praise the Lord. Praise the Lord!
Psalm 150:6 NKJV

Introduction

This story was inspired by Ese (pronounced "essay"), my four-year-old son. Ese took lessons in dance at the Eisenhower Dance Ensemble Center in Rochester, Michigan. Despite being the only boy in the class, he was enthusiastic and found freedom of expression through dance. I know that children all around the world will love dancing through the pages of this book with Ese over and over again!

Ese was a little boy who loved to dance.

He danced in the day with the sun in the sky,
Danced to a chorus of children passing by.

He danced in the night under the moon and stars,
Danced to the rhythms of fireflies in jars.

He danced to the music
of jazz marching bands,

Danced 'round and 'round with cartwheels
and handstands.

He danced with ribbons colorful and bright,
Danced with elegance and fun-filled delight.

He danced catching raindrops from gray clouds above,
Danced under rainbows bursting colors of love.

He danced among flowers swaying in the breeze,
Danced to the songs of birds in the trees.

He danced with butterflies, beautiful and free,
Danced to the beat of his heart's melody.

He danced and danced 'til Mother called his name,
And in dreams after bedtime, Ese danced the same.

listen|imagine|view|experience

AUDIO BOOK DOWNLOAD INCLUDED WITH THIS BOOK!

In your hands you hold a complete digital entertainment package. In addition to the paper version, you receive a free download of the audio version of this book. Simply use the code listed below when visiting our website. Once downloaded to your computer, you can listen to the book through your computer's speakers, burn it to an audio CD or save the file to your portable music device (such as Apple's popular iPod) and listen on the go!

How to get your free audio book digital download:

1. Visit www.tatepublishing.com and click on the e|LIVE logo on the home page.
2. Enter the following coupon code:
   82b7-5b65-1e8a-a865-b6e5-6ab1-11a8-999a
3. Download the audio book from your e|LIVE digital locker and begin enjoying your new digital entertainment package today!